SARFER

DANIEL ARTHUR SMITH

SARFER

Edited By
Crystal Watanabe

Cover and Illustrations By
Ben Adams

Also Written by Daniel Arthur Smith

The Cameron Kincaid Adventures
The Cathari Treasure
The Somali Deception

Literary Fiction
The Potter's Daughter
Opening Day: A Short Story

Horror Fiction
Agroland

Science Fiction
Hugh Howey Lives

~*~

For Susan, Tristan, & Oliver, as all things are.

~*~

ONE

The roaring grate of metal against sand broke the silence of the night amidst the thunderous ruffling flap of the powered down main. Mattie sailed right to their fire, let the flames announce him loud and proud, his waist hooked to the wire, finger on the trigger of the autohoist. Keen on the dramatic, his approach was rapid turmoil, a storm from the darkness.

The wind was strong so he could bust out quick if need be. He wouldn't have come otherwise. Mattie only sailed on a good wind, only at night, and always alone.

And they only expected him by the wind. What use was a courier on a calm night?

This time, no one took notice.

Mattie sized up the two men across the blaze. They hadn't even given him an upward glance, but he saw why. They shared a canteen, and by their childlike cackles, and the faces they made after each pull, he figured it wasn't water they were drinking. Bad form, these two. They were older than him, thirties maybe, and their shirtless arms were covered in a collage of tattoos detailing their allegiance and history. He read the symbols and swirls as he would a book, particularly those with raised scars.

Since Springston fell there were more of them now. Brigands, gypsies, tribes. Roaming through and setting up where they wouldn't have before, making new alliances, no longer just rebels, but growing concerns.

Mattie did business with all of them, as his father had, no questions asked.

He had no tats or allegiances, and he wore his light leather jacket buckled to the neck for the same reason he wore his ker high to his goggles, to keep his body hidden, his business his own. That the jacket also added a bit of girth to his too-thin frame didn't hurt either. The leather was his father's, as were the smoke-glassed goggles and the double-barreled gun holstered to his thigh. Up on the trampoline, next to the mast so high the tip faded into black, he looked like a force to be reckoned with. At least, that was his intention.

His legs might be useless, but above the hull, he stood tall.

Mattie did all of his business above the hull.

"Get in, get out, don't dally." That's what his father always said.

Except the two on the other side of the fire weren't paying any mind. That made him uneasy. As a matter of discipline, he kept his head forward and let his goggle-covered eyes roam the shadows of the small camp, searching for signs of trouble on the off chance someone would try to jump him. He wasn't concerned about Ballenger, the man he'd come to see. Mattie's vocation had a built-in pass. No client would want to take out the courier. No, his attempt at intimidation, his hand on the butt of the gun holstered to his thigh, was for the drunken rogue that might not be thinking straight. He made sure to carry no temptation on the sarfer, and except for water and an old dive suit, the haul rack was empty. But he was well aware that without his father sewing fresh canvas, his oversized sheets were a treasure of another kind.

The four sarfers parked mast down to his left were empty, and besides the two men at the fire, the only other signs of life in the camp were in two of the three large lamp-lit tents, the yellowed outer walls a theater of silhouettes of those inside.

This was not how it was supposed to go.

When he rode in, the client was to greet him with his package, get down to business, and be done. The thought of having to send these two in for Ballenger, just the idea of his young voice being heard, irritated Mattie.

No words, no delay.

Get in, get out, don't dally.

But these two were oblivious.

There was nothing on the trampoline or in his pocket to toss their way, so he bit his lower lip, raised his chest, hesitated for a second in the brief chance they'd look up, and then cleared his throat. "Ahem."

Nothing.

They were right across from him.

The man on the right had a long scar creasing his cheek from the edge of his mouth. He said something to the man on the left that caused him to burst out laughing. Then Scarface raised the canteen bottom high and took a heavy swig of whatever was inside.

That was the thing about all of these new allegiances, all of the new recruits. No discipline.

Mattie cleared his throat again, this time much louder, throwing his chest wide to send out a deep bass, "Ahem."

The two stopped giggling and glanced up above the flames. The sight of Mattie high up on the hull sent them kicking dust into the fire, backpedaling into the sand.

Their panicked reaction produced a slight grin behind Mattie's ker, but he didn't so much as flinch otherwise. He wasn't about to get himself shot by a surprised drunk. He kept his left hand on the butt of the gun, and then, when he decided it was safe to move, slowly raised his right hand forward in a calming manner. He didn't let go of the gadget box or take his finger off the trigger for the autohoist, but gently hovered his gloved palm in front of him until the two calmed down.

They stopped sputtering, glanced at each other, and then at him.

When he was sure they had their wits about them, he slowly shifted his flat palm toward the lit tents.

Scarface slapped the other's upper arm, sending him up and away to fetch Ballenger. Then, without taking his eyes off Mattie, he raised the canteen to the unscarred side of his mouth and sucked a long draw of courage.

~*~

TWO

One thing that stayed consistent with the old ways was that twinkle in a brigand's eyes. They always had it. It was as telltale as the marks on their arms, particularly the way it flared a bit while sizing you up. Didn't matter if you were working with or for or beside them, they just couldn't help themselves. Scarface's glassy eyes were laced with that twinkle, and something more, most likely because of the alcohol and the fact that Mattie got the drop on him.

As if it could ever be possible to get the drop on someone by sailing a sarfer straight up fireside in the middle of camp.

A wounded pride makes a man as dangerous as any fool. Mattie's father had taught him that as well. *Pride will tempt a man to an action he otherwise should pass on.* His father had been talking about business and racing, but to Mattie it applied to any situation. Most all of what his father taught him did.

Stand sentinel, be one with his sarfer, that was all Mattie needed to do. Keep his head forward, staring out across the camp, not down toward Scarface. No reason to incite him.

The dark lens of Mattie's goggles hid the fact that he was mapping the sky, calculating time. The flames of the fire licked to the west and a spray of sand lashed against a thin exposed strip of his upper cheek. The wind had picked up. He would make miles tonight.

The shadow theater on the side of the tent was about to come to a close. He could see what he determined was

Ballenger's silhouette leading the other pirates and their rectangular parcels to the door, the shadow of the man sent inside bent low, cowering behind the boss.

Mattie tightened his grip on the trap wire that fastened him to the mast.

Ballenger angled out the door toward Mattie's sarfer with an intent momentum, each booted step an attack on the hard pack. The firelight amplified the pirate's chiseled cheeks and chin. Mattie watched the chief brigand's eyes dart left to right, and then left to right again, beyond the camp, out into the darkness, as they searched out whatever else Scarface and his comrade might have let get too close.

Ballenger stopped at the edge of the hull, began to bark orders, and thrust his right arm forward, pointing to where the three black trunks would go.

"Fasten that one there, below the beam, the other there, on the far side." He glanced up at Mattie and said, "And put the smaller case up front, in between."

The six men scrambled up onto the trampoline and wasted no time tying down the three black boxes. Mattie would reset the weight a mile or two out, but it was Ballenger's job to get the packages on.

Even with the ker, the smell of the six men bustling so close was worse than a slit trench latrine.

When the pirates finished strapping the cases to the sarfer, they dropped to the sides and headed back to the tent.

Ballenger waited for them to go, and when Scarface stubbornly remained across the fire, he glared at him in a way that made the fool scurry.

Ballenger had more than a twinkle in his eyes. Something worse, layered. He was in a state of permanent contempt. Something festered deep inside of the old brigand, scarred his innards, corkscrewed them in the same way as the ash and grit sand scars that spiraled down his meaty muscled arms.

Mattie got it. At least, he thought he did. He'd lost his father beneath the wall, and a part of him still festered over it. But he was no pirate. He was just a courier, no questions asked.

"You're early. That's good," Ballenger said. "I expected you tomorrow. Looks like you've got the wind."

Mattie heard what Ballenger was really saying – that the wind had come early. They only expected him by the wind. A courier on a calm night was useless.

"There's two cases," Ballenger continued, "though I 'spose you see that. To make up for the load there's more in your case."

Ballenger held his stare at Mattie.

Mattie didn't move. Didn't nod.

"It's not double," Ballenger said. "But it's one and a half your rate, and it's prime."

Nothing.

"Thought you'd wanna stay light."

Again nothing. His father taught him to barter this way. Say nothing and let the client talk himself up. Most men did and Ballenger was no different.

Ballenger's eyes darted to the left and right again. "You'll get the other half on the return."

Mattie twirled the autohoist gadget box in his hand, a signal to let Ballenger move on.

Ballenger tightened his lips and then said, "You're going north, to the wastes. I marked it in wax on your paper. You'll see." He lifted his head to survey the sky. "Keeps up like this, you'll make good time."

Mattie squeezed the trigger against the gadget box and with a loud ruffle and rattle, the battery operated autohoist shot the oversized canvases of the mainsheet and the jib up the twenty-five foot mast, leaving Ballenger on the other side. The autohoist was an invention of his father's, a modification of a winch, which he'd engineered to fit one of two wind generators on the sarfer. It had one job and it performed it well: hoist the sheets fast. With its taste of wind, the canvas lifted the sarfer forward, away from the camp and into the night.

~*~

THREE

Because Ballenger said north, Mattie went west with the wind, playing odds that if anyone were waiting for him in the northerly direction, he'd avoid them. Plus, apart from a gypsy camp eight miles out, the sands west of Ballenger were clear.

He'd head to the trough he'd tacked across on his sail in, then follow it to the hard pack flats before turning north. That was the safest bet. It was also the quickest way to put the brigands behind him. Something about that camp bothered him, like the way Ballenger's eyes probed the night when he spoke, watching for something. Waiting, maybe. Mattie didn't want to fret too much on who or what the hardened man was searching for. Most likely Ballenger thought somebody might not want those cases his men put on the trampoline to get to their destination. They certainly were heavy, and Mattie had noted that it took two of his men to carry each one. But robbers and pirates weren't Mattie's greatest concern. It was marauders, a breed worse than brigand, worse than the cannibals of the north. Marauders were the cannibals that hunted. They were rumored to travel at night, and there was talk that they had expanded their territory.

He'd never seen them. Not many had.

But he'd come across signs of them, father north. There was that sarfer he came across once, dead on the dunes. It was midafternoon when he came upon it, parked mast up on the side of a dune, the main half fallen, ruffling in the breeze.

8

When he first saw it, he thought someone forgot to fly their dive flag. You don't just abandon a sarfer, not one in that good a condition. It was when he drew up close that he saw the signs. Rusty bloodstains spattered across the sail and trampoline, the dried, crackled pool in the cockpit. Blood but no body. It could've been pirates, but pirates take bounty, and the haul rack was full of quality loot. He was sure it was marauders.

That didn't stop him from the runs, though. Most anyone worth their water could map to the stars, but few were familiar enough with the terrain to travel by night.

He trusted his wits.

His father had taught him the sands while delivering canvas, and when the wall fell, Mattie rode the wind out to the brigands. One day he would take to sewing canvas like his father, and his grandfather. He'd start trading sheets again, but until that day came, he was a sarfer for hire, regardless of who else was out there. The great wall had been the safest place in the world, and that was gone now. If he stayed on the hull, kept his mind true, he reckoned he'd be as safe as any.

He tapped the second trigger of the gadget box to give himself some slack on the trap wire and then folded the knees of his useless legs onto the back of the trampoline. He scanned the tops of the dunes and made ready to move if need be. If a tip of a mast broke the star line, he would hoist the third sail and launch with the wind.

The autohoist was only one mod. Mattie had the sarfer of a sailmaker's son. His father was no lord, but had plenty of coin and merch to trade. Mattie didn't have a cockpit the way other sarfers did, just a huge trampoline of a deck. His sarfer was modified for speed, agility, and most of all, modified to compensate for his lame legs. His mast was a third higher than most others and he had the sheets to hoist to it, three of them. That much sail teased right would lift the hulls onto the foils at the slightest breeze. He could glide across the hard pack as easy as if it were lathered with goat fat. He thought back about doing just that, sitting cross-legged on the back, right next to the boom, arm on the tiller. Gliding past the marina, no shirt, just his goggles and ker.

That was forever ago, when there were girls to watch him.

Mattie didn't sail like that anymore.

He missed the girls. The girls of Springston, and girls like Esme out in Pike. She was a beauty, and always saved a special smile just for him. Like all of the small towns to the west, Pike was growing, made it tough to get close, but easy to blend in. He would head out that way after the run. He had some potatoes he'd stashed away and some strawberries too. Esme liked strawberries.

He squinted, keen on the horizon. He was surrounded by nothing but tides of sand and a sea of starlight, the only sound the constant whir of the wind generators and the hiss of the foils against the belly of the trough below. He gave himself a bit more slack on the wire, and then leaned forward to inspect the small case the brigands had placed by the mast. Mattie liked to keep things simple, in exchange for a case of food, water, and coin, he'd haul one case, could be heavy or light, full or near empty, no questions asked.

But Ballenger had sent his men up with two cases, one more than was bargained for, so Mattie was curious what the payment for this prime payload would be

He tapped the small pin from the latch and then tossed the lid back on its hinge. He grabbed the diving visor from the haul rack and flicked on the light.

It was all the same stuff but there was more than usual. Hard bread, a few cans he doubted were anything special, some nuts. The purse on the side was a bit plump. He bit into a piece of the hard bread and then weighed the coin bag in his hand. There was more coin than usual, which was good. Every coin brought him closer to his own shop. He let loose the purse and picked up the map from the side of the box. The map, sealed between sheets of plastic, had his father's mark in the corner. Clients would travel to Springston and with an ash pencil, mark where the delivery would be. Mattie had kept his father's system. His clients still marked where he was to go and he could see in the visor light that Ballenger had indeed marked his destination.

~*~

FOUR

The moon was golden and so was the sand. The trough that ran west was wide, and the wind funneling through intense. Strong enough, Mattie decided, to hoist the third sail, the one his father had called a spinnaker. It was his favorite mod to the craft he now called home. When that front sheet bubbled out and the runners lifted from the sand, it was only then he felt normal, happy. Sure, the trapeze system his father designed raised him high enough to stand, but it made him feel like a puppet on a string, dangling beneath the mast.

Riding the side of the hull put him in control.

When he was a small child, his father would toss him into the air, and it was that same weightlessness he longed for, the brief moments of freedom.

Mattie plopped each of his dead legs straight, then slid over onto the hull. The runners beneath him vibrated up into his spine, sending a quiver through him, a million tingles that forced a smile.

With exhilaration, came action.

He wrapped his hand tight onto the crossbar and with a pelvic thrust locked his left boot into the stirrup, sucked in a breath, and with a hard shove pivoted perpendicular out over the side to the deafening hiss of the foils and the relentless pelting of spraying sand.

The trough rushed by, inches beneath him, while above, the silhouette of the mast and mainsheet cut against the starry sky.

He squeezed his gloves tight and clenched his teeth as another hundred joys coursed through him. No matter how many times he did this, his stomach still tumbled.

Mattie loosened his shoulders and triggered his third sail.

The lines in his hands hummed with new tension as the loud flapping front sheet soared up into place.

He flexed his shoulders and the front sail gently adjusted.

The hull let loose from the earth.

Too soon.

A panic seized his gut. He sharply dipped his shoulders back toward the speeding sand to ease the sarfer level again, and then began to slowly feed the line once more. Gradually the hull rose again, but this time he was ready. He held the front sail steady as he rose high above the trampoline. As he left the trough, the mast lowered to greet it, until the tip was mere feet from the sand and he'd gone from horizontal to near vertical, sarfing by the sheets.

Comfortable with the lines, he began to jibe. The sarfer reacted quickly, racing up the side of the trough, leaving a high rooster tail spew of sand behind.

The sarfer flew past the trough's rim, fully airborne above the dunes.

The full body quiver returned. Mattie was truly riding on the wind and in that instant of utter lightness his legs no longer mattered. He was no slave to gravity, he defied it. It tickled, caused him to laugh beneath his ker. He let out a loud howl. This was his father's gift.

He let the sail take more wind and relaxed his shoulders. Treating the lines as reins, he weaved through the wide belly of the trough. The muscles in his forearms felt strong and he was glad to have an easy path forward. And it was easy, for another hour, until he saw two masts poking above the starboard horizon.

~*~

FIVE

The two sarfers had been hidden by his mainsheet, but he saw them now, between the front sails and mast. Two double-sheeted triangles, skimming above the trough, jutting up and down as they pounded the swells of each dune in turn.

They were marauders.

Mattie had to lose them.

In the distance, he spotted the slow incline, the smooth, angled ramp of the dune that would be his escape.

Any rapid movement would be a flag and they would be on him. So he let the sail out slowly. The line vibrated and pulled back across his knuckle as the moon-bathed sheet hungrily swallowed more wind.

As his sails swelled, the tips of the masts up above began to fall behind.

The ramp was coming up fast.

Mattie's darting eyes turned his head forward to back, from the ramp to his tail.

Then the marauders, first one, then the other, flew from the high rim and gracefully spun forward midair to gently plant down in the trough.

Growing up in Springston, he'd never come across anyone that could maneuver as well as him, and now these two agile pilots were effortlessly closing in. So close that he could see the front-runner's menacingly blank goggles beaming toward him, black voids beneath a shadowy skullcap.

Mattie broke away from the shadowy pursuer to focus on the approaching ramp. With some intuitive mental math, he calculated the angle of the mainsheet and jib needed to force the turn.

Driven by sail, the leeward hull sliced through the sand to the ramp, out of the trough, and high into the air.

Beneath Mattie, the cool tan sands spread out for miles in every direction.

He was at his best weightless, when the fight with gravity was at its least. Intuitively, he manipulated the canvas to do his bidding, touching down on the next incline without loss of momentum.

He was one with the wind.

Unfortunately, a flash of canvas in the corner of his eye showed him that the marauders were just as wily with their short-hulled sarfers as he was with his modified one.

There was no easy escape. If he could make it to the hard pack flats to the west, he could go full sheet and then maybe break free.

But the flats were miles of sand and wind from the dunes he was dancing. If his skills stayed true, he'd be fine, but one folly and they'd be on him.

~*~

SIX

The beam swung hard, close and then away. The golden moon and the crystalline stars swiveled around him with each maneuver as he flew with the wind, spinning the sarfer midair to tackle each dune and hollow.

With every rise above the sand, he could see the marauders tight on his tail, doggedly holding pursuit.

The canvas popped and the lines fought back. His arms began to ache. How long had it been since they came upon him – tens of minutes, an hour – he was not sure. The dune dance had become redundant, each tack a mirror of the last. It was only a matter of time before he pulled the beam too far and lost wind, or worse, the too soft side of a dune would suck him in.

The marauders had his course to follow, the advantage of his lead. Even if Mattie made no mistake, there would be a point where one of the two would spy an opening, cut in close, and steal his wind. He'd used the same tactic racing with other boys in Springston. His father had taught him. Send your partner in slow to rob them of their wind and then circle around for the lead, except these were no boys and this was no race. They'd circle around to finish him.

But the memory triggered another. The thought of a tactic he could use.

He let the sarfer fall into the deep valley of the next dune, leaned far back into the trap wire that suspended him, and when he felt the shallow crosswind, pulled the beam hard.

The sarfer spun.

Mattie's head whapped against the side of the dune, pounding sand over and onto him.

The maneuver was crazy, a spin in the hollow. He could have wiped out. Should have.

But as the craft reached a one-eighty, the crosswind bit and launched him back the way he came.

Mattie's gamble on the switchback paid off.

He clenched the bar tightly with his forward hand, and with the other, he unholstered his father's gun and flung the heavy barrel onto the crossbar.

There were two large shells loaded, one in each of the double barrels. He'd paid well for them, but they were untested and he had no idea if either would fire.

As he angled up the high dune, he gained speed, a lot of speed, enough to launch him up and, by chance, into the full sails of the leading marauder.

The angle of the collision spared his hull. He smashed the marauder's mast, shearing it from his sarfer.

As he plowed overhead, he swung the barrel of the gun up, over, and behind him.

The pilot, a thin-framed shadow, had been knocked forward onto the side of his cockpit. Mattie centered the barrels and squeezed the first trigger.

Mattie's shoulder jerked back as thunder and flame erupted from the end of the gun. The shadow man convulsed in a death throe.

Mattie whirled his torso around to correct his canvas, but he was too late. The bow of his sarfer ate into the side of the next dune. With a tremendous jolt, the roaring rush of wind went silent, then a squeal of rubbing metal filled the air as his mast collapsed back on its hinge. Momentum first thrust him forward, and then the tall pole jerked the wire at his waist, flinging him into the sand.

Mattie's head took the brunt of the landing and his goggles smashed into his face as he plowed the surface of the dune ear deep.

He frantically shoved the earth away, thrusting himself onto his back. Still blinded, he tore the goggles up from his face. Above him, a thin haze of fuchsia banded the center third of the sky, punctuated by millions of points of crystal bright white. And then, eerily slow, the sky above Mattie disappeared, eclipsed by the square front of the second marauder's sarfer.

The gun was still in his hand. Without a second thought, Mattie bent his elbow to raise the barrel of the heavy gun upright and squeezed.

Again an explosion showered from the tip of the barrel. Above him, a small fist-sized portal of starlight burst open beneath the soaring craft.

And then the marauder disappeared from his line of sight, over the dune, leaving Mattie alone with the golden moon, the blowing sand, and the voice of his father.

~*~

SEVEN

Mattie gazed out at the sand scrapers beyond the studio wall to the glittering tin roofs of the shantytown. In the year since he'd become a captive in the great wall he'd grown attached to the dwellings beyond the edge of Springston. Mostly he enjoyed watching the sarfers come into the far-off marina, one less civil than what laid below the great wall. They would fly in full sail, breaking only at the last. If he let himself gaze long enough, the crutches no longer cut into his armpits, his legs were no longer lame.

Mattie's father drew his attention to the bench beside him with a series of wispy blows. He was blasting air onto a buckle to clear any grains of sand lodged in the crease of the leather. Despite its height, the huge loft could not escape the constant micro drifts that creeped out from every crevice. When he was finished puffing, Liam rubbed the metal with his thick polishing cloth and lifted it from the workbench up to the windowed wall. It gleamed yellow in the afternoon sun. Mattie enjoyed being with his father while he worked. He'd been at the end of the bench, his weight on his crutches, waiting for his father to finish the rigging. The way Liam's eyes went soft when he examined a piece, as if it were the only thing in existence, pleased Mattie. The quirky way he sucked up his cheek, poking the tip of his tongue in and out of the side of his mouth until he got whatever object just right, and then the light, rising grin that signaled satisfaction with the work he'd done. With every piece, the whole process repeated. But the results were always the same: fine work.

And the rig he'd just finished was fine, too.

The straps were cut from a new piece of finely tanned goat leather and fastened with bright buckles a client brought in for payment.

Liam spread the top belt of the new rigging wide with his fingertips and lifted it to his chest. A long strap on either side held another belt of the same size that hung below it. From that one, two smaller hoops dangled.

"I like it," Mattie said.

"Do you know what is?"

Liam often quizzed his son on the components of the sail, where to double stitch, the working of the blocks that held the lines, all of the parts of a sarfer. Mattie used to enjoy the game more when he thought of himself as his father's protégé. But he could barely drag himself across the studio with his metal crutches, much less lower himself to the floor to mend a sail. He didn't have to think too long or too hard about it before seeing the whole picture. With his lower spine damaged, there was little chance he'd take over his father's studio.

Still, his father was far more optimistic and continued the game regardless of circumstances too obvious to anyone else, so Mattie played along. He didn't recognize what his father had put together, but he had an idea. "I don't know the name," he said, "but I know what it's for. The small hoops fasten to the mast and the larger ones tie the main."

Liam's face told him that he could be right, but he

wasn't.

Mattie pursed his lips.

"Take another guess," his father had said. Liam was always patient.

"If it's not for tying the sails, I don't know what it is."

"It's not for the sails. It's for you. It's a harness."

Mattie had not even thought of such a purpose for the rigging, but he saw it now. The top belts were for his waist and chest and the bottom hooped belts were for his legs. "What am I supposed to do with that?"

"I think it's time you started piloting again."

Had he the courage, Mattie would have glared at his father. Instead, he dropped his gaze. It would be cruel to be mad.

"It's been almost a year since the accident," Liam said. "You're healed. It's time you got back up."

"What's the point? I'm not going to race again. My legs are useless."

"Do you remember when you were little and we took the Cannondale to the top of the Aurora dune?"

Mattie did remember that pleasant day. He couldn't have been more than five. His father had taken Mattie and his mother out on the sarfer to the large Aurora dune. He brought with them the Cannondale. The Cannondale was a tall, aluminum, tube-framed ski bike with a seat, handlebars, and a single sarfer runner fixed to its bottom. They'd named the ski bike Cannondale because the odd word was painted across the main support strut. They had spent the day coasting the ski bike down the hill. Mattie remembered his feet could not touch the ground. His father held the bike for him at the top of the dune and sent him off with a run. It was one of the best days of his life.

"Sure."

"Do you remember how many times you fell over sideways going down the dune until you figured out how to balance the bike between your legs?" Now that he mentioned it, Mattie did remember. The visions in his mind of coasting down the dune were sprinkled with a series of wipeouts.

Mattie chuckled. "I remember I fell a lot until I got it right."

"Uh huh. And do you remember what I told you?"

"You said that when you fall down, you get back up."

"That's right. You're moving along fine on those crutches. Now it's time for you to get back up."

He couldn't argue with his father. His heart wasn't into defying such a kind man, a man that didn't see him as damaged. Still he contested. "There is no way I can drive a sarfer. I drag my feet with these." He hefted the crutches an inch from the floor to make his point. They landed with a thud.

"One thing has nothing to do with the other. When you fall down, you get back up. And as long as I'm here, I'll help you. Let's get this on."

"But I don't see—"

"You will," his father said.

Liam first buckled the belt around Mattie's waist, then fastened the straps around each leg, then his chest.

Mattie had nil movement in his legs, but he had some feeling. The harness was snug, comfortable. "Okay. What now?" Mattie asked.

"Now wait a minute."

Liam walked toward a curtain that spanned the end of the studio. A curtain hung on either side of the loft, one to shield off the cots they used as beds, and this one for his father's tools and projects in various states of completion. His father pushed the canvas open with a stride across the room. The wire rings suspending the curtain scraped across the cable. Behind it was a hoist frame, a tall metal pole with a protruding arm near the ceiling holding a hoist on the end. He grabbed the hoist controller and tapped one of the triggers of the control box. Nothing. Liam came back toward Mattie.

"What are you doing?" Mattie asked.

Liam laughed and picked up a battery from the bench. "I forgot this."

He returned to the hoist frame, installed the battery near the small motor at the bottom, and then took the controller in hand again. This time the hoist came to life and began to roll across the floor.

Mattie saw another piece of new rigging dangling from the end of the wire. "You're going to hoist me up?"

"Pretty much."

When the hoist frame reached Mattie, it stopped. There was a ring with a bungee attached. Liam clasped the line to his son's harness. "We'll have to tweak this a bit," he said.

"What do you call this?"

"It's called a trapeze. Here, take the control box and hit that trigger."

Mattie took the box in hand. He'd used the hoist before, but his father had tampered with the controller. There were extra triggers on the side. He tapped the one Liam had pointed to. The crutch below that arm fell away as his body jerked upward.

"Whoa," Mattie said.

Liam grabbed his son's sides to balance him and said with a smile, "We'll have to tweak that too, I guess."

~*~

EIGHT

The new rigging worked marvelously. It had not taken Mattie long to get used to the line he'd taken to calling the 'trap,' and he now had the freedom to lose the crutches, at least in the loft. He and Liam had made a few adjustments to the hoist and the box, and after a few setbacks, Mattie found a way to maneuver around in ways he couldn't even when his legs worked. With a shift of his weight and the tap of a trigger, he could bring himself down horizontally above a canvas on the floor. The key was the addition of braces to his legs that he could lock in place with a slight pelvic thrust, giving his legs a purpose he could leverage again. What craftsmen would have thought to hang inches above the work as opposed to kneeling all day? He was able to get in close without disrupting the sail, and the sails he was working on were huge. His father had an idea that in order for the trap to work on a sarfer the mast would have to be extra high, and a tall mast meant tall sails. There would be three of them, a main, a jib, and a spinnaker. Not many sarfers had a third sail. But his father had a plan, and an idea as to how to hoist them.

~*~

NINE

By the time the last of the specialized parts were finished, Mattie was moving around the studio as fluidly as anyone with legs. He seldom left the loft and the hoist. Leaving the hoist meant the loss of his newfound mobility and dependence on his metal crutches. So when Liam told him that the sarfer had been assembled in the marina below, and that it was time to leave the great wall, Mattie was less than enthusiastic. He put his weight on the metal poles he'd so eagerly discarded and began his descent down from the loft. Each step a jolt to his upper body and his ego.

When they finally reached the marina, Liam told Mattie to wait while he talked to the dockmaster. Mattie recognized many of the faces aboard the Sarfers moving in and out. Each that passed by shared a smile with the sailmaker's son. He pushed his shoulders up, extending himself as tall as he could. But regardless of his posturing, the reflection he saw in the eyes of the marina patrons was that of pity for a broken boy, prompting a rush through his chest and causing his throat to tighten and dry.

That his legs could not race him away only added to his grief.

He fought to smile at his father when he saw him exit the tall Quonset hut he used as his marina workspace. His father walked fifteen feet from the opening and then waved to someone still inside, beckoning them to come to him as he stepped backward.

Within a few seconds two dock hands emerged, each pulling a line, and then behind them came their toil, a sarfer, larger than any Mattie had seen before. Its hulls were thick and long and the folded-back mast was the length of a flagpole.

Mattie's anxiety was forgotten, quickly replaced by the exhilaration of seeing the product of his last few months' work. Each piece had passed through the hands of he and his father, the sails, riggings, and blocks, up in the loft, the sarfer itself in the workshop.

The dock hands dragged the new craft to a slab of flat sand and then secured the dock lines they held to the mooring posts.

The tips of his crutches tore through the sand as he raced to the sarfer. His father went to work raising the mast, and when Mattie reached him, he was ready with the trap wire.

Weeks of maneuvering around the studio, hooked to the hoist, had prepared him for this. Mattie clipped himself into the large ring and hit the trigger that would raise him onto the trampoline, up next to the high-poled mast. The marina shrunk around him. For the first time in over a year he was back on a sarfer, feeling tall above the hulls.

"Hit the next trigger," his father said.

Mattie did. A sucking sound ran through the tall mast and the main sheet shot up.

"Whoa!" Mattie exclaimed. Liam had done it. Just like he said he would.

"What do you think?" his father asked.

"Are you kidding? I'm never getting off this thing."

~*~

TEN

Mattie felt a trickle of sweat run from his forehead down behind his ear. The back of his head was damp and the inside was spinning as blood settled down from his body sprawled uphill. The golden moon had been above the dune when he'd fallen, now the sandy crest hid half of it. The foul odor of the gun's spent shells hung in the air. He could taste the burnt gunpowder through his ker, faintly metallic in his mouth. He hadn't thought of moving. His body ached, the slam against the dune, the firing of his father's gun. His mind had drifted.

Drifted to his father and the mantra that had taught him as a child to persevere, a mantra that had saved him from his crutches, from the loft, the mantra that had saved him from the fall of Springston and given him a vocation, and the opportunity to build a studio of his own.

"When you fall down, you get back up."

He was unsure if he heard the words aloud or in his head. His eyes, glazed from staring, slowly came to life, began searching the sky above him for the face of his father.

"What do you when you fall down?" he heard his father ask. "Get back up," Mattie mouthed into the silent night.

A star darted across the sky. Mattie tensed his forehead, focused his eyes. He remembered a shooting and a falling star were one and the same. That one though, appeared to be alive, soaring so fast and direct, drawing a line with its fiery tail.

"What do you when you fall down?" his father asked again.

With a soft gasp, Mattie said, "Get back up."

Another star darted across the sky. And then another, and another, painting the late night with streaks of lemon and tangerine. "Meteors," he said aloud.

He bent his neck up toward the moonlit sarfer. His feet were below where the edge of the trampoline and the still sheeted mast met.

He sucked in a deep breath and again said, "When you fall down, you get back up." And then he reached out his arm and lunged forward to take hold of the sheet.

His hand swung over and missed. The mast was farther than he'd thought. His gut was tight from his own weight, the muscles burning, yet he crunched harder, swiping at the canvas until his finger clutched the edge of the fabric. He leaned in hard and dragged himself closer, and when his body was near enough, he tossed the gun up onto the trampoline and used both hands to pull himself up with it.

He paused on the deck to catch his breath and then rolled onto his back. Showers of light filled the sky. *A celebration*, he thought, just for him.

He sat up. Above the hull, he was back at home. The pilot of the other sarfer still lay dead in his broken craft. Mattie was sure the same was true of the other marauder that had disappeared over the dune. He shuffled himself across the craft to inspect his own mast. He was lucky. The sudden stop had jarred it, nothing more. He unhooked the trap from himself and fastened it to a metal ring on the front of the hull.

He tapped the trigger of the gadget box and the towering mast lifted into place.

The forward sheets ruffled loudly, and then the sarfer lifted.

~*~

~*~

THE
END

~*~

.

ABOUT THE AUTHOR

Daniel Arthur Smith is the author of the international bestsellers **HUGH HOWEY LIVES, THE CATHARI TREASURE, THE SOMALI DECEPTION**, and a few other novels and short stories.

He was raised in Michigan and graduated from Western Michigan University where he studied philosophy, with focus on cognitive science, meta-physics, and comparative religion. He began his career as a bartender, barista, poetry house proprietor, teacher, and then became a technologist and futurist for the Fortune 100 across the Americas and Europe.

Daniel has traveled to over 300 cities in 22 countries, residing in Los Angeles, Kalamazoo, Prague, Crete, and now writes in Manhattan where he lives with his wife and young sons.

For more information, visit danielarthursmith.com

~*~

www.ingramcontent.com/pod-product-compliance
Lightning Source LLC
Chambersburg PA
CBHW020608130626
46552CB00007B/3105